This Book
Belongs To:

Clarissa Quach

THE THREE LITTLE KITTENS
AND OTHER STORIES

from the
Best Loved Stories Collection

Copyright © 2004 by Dalmatian Press, LLC

All rights reserved
Printed in the U.S.A.

Cover Design by Bill Friedenreich

The DALMATIAN PRESS name and logo are trademarks
of Dalmatian Press, LLC, Franklin, Tennessee 37067.
No part of this book may be reproduced or copied in any form
without the written permission of Dalmatian Press.

ISBN: 1-40370-750-2
13142-0604

04 05 06 07 08 LBM 10 9 8 7 6 5 4 3 2 1

Best Loved Stories Collection

THE THREE LITTLE
KITTENS

AND OTHER STORIES

 DALMATIAN PRESS

Table of Contents

The Three Little Kittens

Retold by Jackie Andrews

Illustrated by Lawrie Taylor

Once there were three little kittens called Daisy, Maisy and Bo. They lived with their mother in a tiny house on top of a hill.

One day, a parcel arrived from grandmother.

Inside were three new coats; a blue coat for
Daisy, a red coat for Maisy and a yellow coat for
Bo. The three kittens put them on.

"Meow! Aren't we smart?" they cried.

"Yes, indeed," purred their mother. "I'll have to knit you all some mittens, now, to wear with your new coats."

She finished them that very week: blue mittens for Daisy, red mittens for Maisy and yellow mittens for Bo. The three little kittens were very happy and proud of their new outfits.

"Take care of your mittens, won't you?" said their mother. "Be sure you don't lose them!"

Day after day, the three little kittens wore their mittens every time they left the house. But one day, catastrophe! They ran to their mother with tears in their eyes.

"Mama, Mama!" they cried. "We've lost our mittens. Whatever shall we do?"

Their mother was busy making a delicious blackberry pie. She turned to look at her three kittens and frowned. "You've lost your mittens? You naughty kittens!" she scolded. "Then you shall have no pie."

"Meow!"

Daisy, Maisy and Bo wiped their eyes and
blew their noses on their handkerchiefs.
Then they went to look for their mittens.

First, they went to the chicken coop, where a
fat brown hen was sitting on her eggs.

"Have you seen our mittens, Clucky Hen?"
they asked.

"Cluck, cluck, cluck," said Clucky Hen. "No, I
haven't seen your mittens. Have you looked in
your pockets?"

Daisy, Maisy and Bo pulled everything out of
their pockets and shook their heads.

"Meow! No mittens there," they said.

Next, the three little kittens searched their bedroom. They looked in all the cupboards and drawers, and under all the beds.

"Meow! No mittens there!"

Then they climbed up into the attic to look in a chest full of old clothes.

"This is a silly place to look," said Bo. "We haven't been up here in ages."

But it was good fun, exploring.

They tried hard to remember all the places they had been in the last two days.

"We've only been to the wood to pick blackberries," said Maisy.

"And that's where they are!" cried Daisy. "They're hanging on the bushes!"

"That's right," said Bo. "We took them off to pick the blackberries."

The three little kittens scooted away to the
wood. And there were the red, blue and yellow
mittens, hanging from the blackberry bushes
just where they had left them.

The kittens snatched them up and ran home
to tell their mother.

"Put on your mittens, you silly kittens," she
said with a laugh, "and you shall have some pie."

"This is the tastiest blackberry pie I've ever eaten," said Maisy.

"It's the juiciest blackberry pie I've ever eaten," said Daisy.

"Oh no!" said Bo. "Just look at our mittens!"

The three little kittens ran to show their mother their messy, sticky mittens.

"Meow! What shall we do?" they cried.

"You must wash your mittens," said their mother, "and hang them out to dry. Then they'll be as good as new."

Maisy fetched the washtub. Daisy found the laundry soap. Bo brought the clothes pins and the laundry basket. They filled the washtub with warm water. Then they tipped in some soap powder and swished it round to make bubbles.

In went their mittens.

Wash, wash, wash, went the three little kittens until all the blackberry stains had disappeared and their mittens were bright blue, red and yellow again.

They hung them on the clothes-line to dry.

"Look, Mama!" The three little kittens held up their soft, fluffy mittens. Daisy wore blue, Maisy wore red and Bo wore yellow.

Their mother smiled at them.

"Such clean mittens," she said, "and such clever kittens. You've had a very busy day. It's time for three little kittens to be fast asleep now."

Daisy, Maisy and Bo climbed into their basket and snuggled up together. Soon they were fast asleep and dreaming of blackberry pie.

Purr, purr, purr.

The Three Little Kittens

Three little kittens, they lost their mittens,
And they began to cry,
Oh, Mother dear, we sadly fear
That we have lost our mittens.
What! Lost your mittens, you naughty kittens!
Then you shall have no pie!
Meow, meow, meow,
No, you shall have no pie!
The three little kittens, they found their mittens,
And they began to cry,
Oh, Mother dear, see here, see here,
For we have found our mittens.
Put on your mittens, you silly kittens,
And you shall have some pie.
Purr, purr, purr,
Oh, let us have some pie.

The End

The Donkey
and
the Lapdog

Retold by Val Biro

Illustrated by Val Biro

Once there was a man who had a house and a farm. The house was filled with nice tables and chairs and the farm produced lots of lovely things to eat. The man was very proud of his house and farm.

He also had a donkey and a lapdog. Both animals had four legs, but otherwise they were very different.

The donkey worked hard all day on the farm. He was very good at it. He always had plenty of food and he slept in the stable at night.

It was a warm and comfortable stable, but the donkey kept thinking about the lapdog.

"I cart and carry all day long," he said to himself, "while that silly dog has an easy life with everybody making a fuss of him!"

This was perfectly true because the lapdog played all day in the house, and he was very good at it. So good, in fact, that everybody fussed over and petted him and he didn't do a stroke of work.

He just enjoyed himself all day and he slept in a soft bed at night, a real doggy bed, right by the side of his master.

At mealtimes he would do what he could do best of all; he would sit on people's laps. That's why he was called a lapdog. He sat on his master's lap at dinner, and he had lovely things to eat. What a lucky dog!

The donkey looked through the window and he was very jealous.

"That dog must be very clever," he thought, "to have all that fussing and petting and all that lovely food without having to do any work for it."

The donkey said, "I wish I could be more like the dog. The farmer and his wife would make a pet of me and I would do nothing but play all day."

So one day he trotted into the house and began to play just like the dog.

He jumped and capered around the room, but he upset the table and chairs. He was far too big and clumsy. Soon the room was a mess.

"Never mind!" the donkey thought and he tried to bark just like the little lapdog, but all he could say was "HEE-HAW!"

Then he saw the lovely things to eat. He
jumped up on his master's lap, just like the dog.

"That should do the trick," thought the donkey.

"Now my master will fuss over me and pet
me and give me lovely food for being such a

good lapdog."

But the master would have none of this! He was very angry. He jumped up, shouting, "You clumsy brute! What do you think you are doing? You're a donkey, not a lapdog!"

He grabbed a broom and chased the donkey
back to the stable. The master's wife ran after
the donkey and the master, shaking her rolling-
pin, and the lapdog ran after them all!

"HEE-HAW, HEE-HAW!" brayed the donkey
as he ran back to his stable.

The donkey decided he had been silly to pretend to be a lapdog. Lapdogs were silly and useless. It was better to be a donkey, doing donkey work, eating donkey food, and sleeping in a donkey stable.

"I am no good at being a lapdog," said the donkey. "I will just be a donkey."
And he has been a donkey ever since, which is what he had been best at being all along.

The End

The Goose and the Golden Eggs

Retold by Val Biro

Illustrated by Val Biro

A man and his wife had a goose. They lived in a cottage and the goose lived in the yard. The man and his wife were poor. They grumbled all day and wished all the time to be rich.

"I wish we had a bigger house," said the man, sighing.

His wife agreed. "I wish I had some sparkling jewels," she said.

The man sighed again. "And I wish I had a bag of gold," he said.

One day the goose laid a golden egg. It lay on the ground sparkling and glittering.

"Look at that," called his wife. The man could hardly believe his eyes. He snatched up the egg. It was smooth and large and heavy.

"It is solid gold!" he shouted.

"It is worth a fortune!" cried his wife. They danced round and round in excitement.

"We shall be rich!" they shouted. And they danced around again thinking of bags of gold and piles of jewels, until they were quite exhausted.

The man and his wife could hardly wait until market day to sell the egg and buy all the things they wanted.

Then the goose laid another golden egg.

"Just think," said the wife. "If our goose goes on laying a golden egg each day, we shall become the richest people in the village."

"That's going to take a long time," the man said. "I want to be rich now."

"So do I," said his wife. "But what shall we do?"

"The goose must be full of gold," said the man. "If I cut it open, we shall have all the gold now!"

"Yes!" his wife replied. "The goose must be made of gold! Let's open her and see."

So they opened the goose. The man looked inside one half and his wife looked inside the other. They looked at each other and then looked inside the goose again. They could not believe their eyes.

They had expected the goose to be full of gold, but the goose was full of goose!

They had killed the goose for nothing! So the
man and his wife had no more golden eggs, and
no more goose!

They were the silliest people in the village,
because they had killed the goose that laid the
golden eggs.

The End

The Bear and the Travelers

Retold by Val Biro

Illustrated by Val Biro

One day, two friends were traveling together on a lonely road. The road led into a big dark wood near the tall mountains in India. The two friends were completely alone in the silent wood. They were silent too, as they walked along.

One of them was young and the other was old. At last the young man spoke.

"I don't like this place. It feels dangerous. But never mind, we are good friends and if we stick close together, nothing can hurt us."

The old man agreed with his friend and they continued their journey.

Suddenly a brown bear came out of the woods. He was huge and fierce. He looked straight at the two travelers, with a wicked grin on his face.

"Ah-ha!" he growled. "Here comes my dinner!"

He grinned even more, showing his big sharp teeth, and began lumbering toward the two travelers.

The men were afraid and ran away. They had no guns and the old man was too weak to fight the bear with his stick.

The young man was stronger, but he was so frightened that he ran for his life.

The bear chased after them. His big paws

churned up the dust and he was getting nearer and nearer.

The old man knew that he could not run fast enough to get away from the bear, so he called out to his young friend, "Take my stick and fight the bear!"

But the young man ran fast and climbed up a tall tree to hide. He was safe. The old man was slow and could not climb.

Then the old man suddenly remembered being told that a bear will not touch someone who is dead. So he lay down and pretended to be dead. He hoped that what people had said about bears was right, because he knew his friend was not going to help him.

The big brown bear came up and walked all around him. "At least I have half my dinner!" the bear said.

The bear sniffed the old man's feet, then his legs and then his back. The old man stayed very, very still. He shut his eyes tight and held his breath.

The bear thought that there was something wrong, so he went on sniffing. He sniffed the old man's hands, his head and his nose.

Then the bear sniffed at his ear.

"He must be dead," the bear growled. "I never eat dead people." The bear was very cross. Half his dinner was up in a tree where he could not reach it, and the other half lay dead in front of him.

So the bear went away without his dinner. "I am certainly out of luck today," the bear thought.

The old man opened his eyes and saw the bear disappearing into the big dark wood, but he lay very still until it was gone.

When it was safe, the young man in the tree came down. He had seen everything from his hiding place and he wanted to know why the bear had gone away without eating his friend.

He had also seen the bear mutter something before it went away. "What did the bear say when he sniffed at your ear?" he asked his friend.

The old man sat up and got to his feet. He looked sternly at the young man.

"That I should never again travel with a friend who leaves me in danger!" said the old man.

Then the old man turned, and as he walked away he said, "Remember, a true friend will never let you down."

The End

The Great Turnip

Retold by Jackie Andrews

Illustrated by Lawrie Taylor

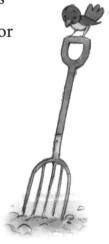

There was once a little old man who lived with his wife in a pretty cottage in the country. He grew wonderful vegetables, which his wife made into delicious stews and pies.

One spring morning, the little old man went out into the garden to plant some turnip seeds. He dug a shallow trench, scattered in the seeds along it, and covered them with soil, patting it down carefully.

Then he put away his tools and went back into the house for a cup of tea.

Days went by and little green shoots popped up out of the ground. The little old man carefully hoed round the young plants, making sure there were no weeds or stones in their way.

So the young turnips grew and grew. But one of them grew much faster than the others. The little old man thinned out some of the other seedlings to give it more room.

The turnip went on growing and growing.
First it was the size of a soccer ball.

Then it was the size of a barrel. And then it
was as large as the wheelbarrow.

And still it grew and grew, until it became a
great big enormous turnip, the size of the little
old man's favorite armchair.

The little old man looked at the great big enormous turnip and thought it was wonderful.

His wife looked at the great big enormous turnip and wondered how it would ever fit into her cooking pot.

One morning the little old man's wife said, "Why don't you pull up that turnip today, so I can make us a nice stew for supper? You don't want it to get old and tough."

Now, the little old man didn't really want to pull up the biggest turnip he had ever grown. But he knew his wife was right: if he left it much longer, the turnip would not taste very good. So, taking his garden fork, he went down to the garden to dig it up.

The little old man dug all round the turnip
to loosen the soil. Then he put his arms
around the huge vegetable, grasped it firmly,
and pulled.

And **pulled** ...

But the great big enormous turnip didn't budge.

"My goodness," said the little old man,
straightening up. "I shall need some help with
this." And he called his wife.

The little old man's wife held her husband firm-ly round the waist. The little old man grasped the great big enormous turnip, and together they pulled.

And *pulled* …

But the great big enormous turnip didn't budge.

"My goodness, husband," said the little old man's wife, "we'll need some help with this." And she called the boy from next door.

The boy next door came and held on to the little old lady. The little old lady held on to her husband and the little old man grasped the great big enormous turnip.

Together they pulled.

And *pulled* ...

But the great big enormous turnip didn't budge.

"We need some more help," said the boy from next door. And he called his sister.

The girl from next door held on to the boy. The boy held on to the little old lady. The old lady held on to her husband, and the little old man grasped the great big enormous turnip. Together they pulled.

And *pulled* ...

But the great big enormous turnip didn't budge.
"We need some more help," said the girl from
next door, and she called the dog.

The dog held on to the girl. The girl held on to the boy. The boy held on to the little old lady. The old lady held on to her husband, and the little old man grasped the great big enormous turnip.

Together they pulled.
And *pulled* …
But the great big enormous turnip didn't budge.
"We need some more help," barked the dog, and he called the cat.

The cat held on to the dog. The dog held on to the girl. The girl held on to the boy. The boy held on to the little old lady. The old lady held on to her husband, and the little old man grasped the great big enormous turnip. Together they pulled.

And *pulled* …

But the great big enormous turnip didn't budge.
"We need some more help," mewed the cat, and
she called the mouse.

The mouse held on to the cat. The cat held on to the dog. The dog held on to the girl. The girl held on to the boy. The boy held on to the little old lady. The old lady held on to her husband, and the little old man grasped the great big enormous turnip. Together they pulled.

And **pulled** ...

And at last, the great big enormous turnip began to move.

The little old man, his wife, the boy from next door, the girl from next door, the dog, the cat and the mouse all tumbled to the ground as the turnip came out of the ground with a great big enormous *sschllluuuuppp.*

That evening, the little old woman cooked a
scrumptious turnip stew for supper.

Then the little old man, the little old woman,
the boy and the girl, the dog, the cat and the
mouse all sat down together at the table and
enjoyed the best meal any of them could
remember.

The End

The
Sick Lion

Retold by Val Biro

Illustrated by Val Biro

It was a hot day. Lion felt too tired to hunt for his dinner. He was getting old and hunting was becoming more and more difficult, especially on a day like this. But he was hungry, so he sat down and began to think.

"How can I look for my dinner without all that running about?" he asked himself. He spent a while deep in thought, and suddenly he had an idea. Lion grinned a very wicked grin.

"I know," he said. "My dinner can come to me."

He went into his den and when he came out again he was wearing his pajamas. Soon all the animals in the forest came to see what was wrong with Lion. They were careful not to get too close to him because lions are dangerous animals.

Lion began to limp. Then he began to shiver, and then he mopped his brow. When he was sure that all the animals were watching him, he turned away. He pretended to be sick and went to bed in his den.

The other animals felt sorry for him. "We must go and visit him," they said. They thought that a sick lion would not be so dangerous. But clever Fox had spied on Lion and seen him grin his wicked grin.

"Take care," warned Fox. "He might eat you."

"Perhaps he's right. Maybe we should not visit Lion," said the others. Rabbit, who was the most timid of all, scampered away and some of the others ran after him.

But Cow was very brave. "You are such cowards," she said. "Poor Lion is sick and I want to cheer him up."

So she went first and knocked at the den door.

"Come in, come in!" called Lion from his bed. He made his voice sound feeble, and the darkness hid his wicked grin.

So Cow went in, but she never came out. All the other animals said how brave Cow was, and did not notice that she never came out of the den.

The next day Pig said, "I will copy Cow and show that I am brave," and he followed Cow's footprints into Lion's den.

The others saw Pig go in through the den door, leaving his own footprints in the sand. The rest of the animals wondered who else would be as brave as Pig.

Goat went in next to copy Pig. But neither Goat nor Pig came out again. Only their footprints remained in the sand.

The next day, Rabbit decided to copy Goat, then Duck waddled after to copy Rabbit. Nobody saw them again.

Clever Fox was watching
everything from a distance.
He had seen all the animals
go into the den to cheer up the sick lion.
"Lion must be feeling very cheerful by now," he
thought, "with all his dinners walking in like that."

Fox stood by the door and called, "How are you, Lion?" Lion was delighted to hear the voice of another visitor. He licked his lips and grinned his wicked grin, but he made his voice sound very feeble.

"Very poorly," said Lion. "Why don't you come in, my friend?" Lion hoped that Fox would copy all the other animals and come in to be eaten, but Fox was too clever for that. He stood by the door and looked at the footprints in the sand.

Fox said, "Because I am not a copycat! I see all these footprints going in, but none coming OUT!"

Fox was too clever to follow all the other animals into the den to be eaten by the lion.

And so Fox stayed out—and Lion was outfoxed!

The End

The Town Mouse and the Country Mouse

Retold by Val Biro

Illustrated by Val Biro

A poor country mouse lived in a ditch. It was just an ordinary ditch, but he had made it quite comfortable.

He enjoyed the peace of the countryside all around him, because he was just an ordinary country mouse.

One day he wrote to an old friend, a rich town mouse, to ask him to dinner. It would be nice to see him again, he thought, and he was sure the town mouse would enjoy the peace and quiet of the countryside.

So he tidied up the ditch, prepared a dinner and waited for his friend to arrive.

The town mouse came. He was very rich and dressed in expensive clothes.

The town mouse and the country mouse sat down to eat a dinner of barleycorn and roots. The town mouse tried a few nibbles but he did not like the dinner and he did not like the country.

At last the town mouse said, "The country is dull. My poor friend, you only eat roots and corn. You should see how I live! You must come to my house in town."

The country mouse had heard exciting tales about town life and the wonderful food to be found there.

The country mouse said, "Thank you for your invitation. I would enjoy the town for a change."

So the town mouse and the country mouse went to town.

The country mouse had never seen so many houses before. They hurried past many fine buildings until they came to the largest house on the street.

"This is my house," said the town mouse proudly.

The town mouse took his friend into the kitchen pantry.

The country mouse had never seen anything like it. There was cheese and honey! There were figs and apples, nuts and dates.

"This is better than barleycorn and roots," thought the country mouse.

The town mouse and the country mouse sat down to dinner. The country mouse was very hungry and he reached out for a piece of cheese.

Just then a man came in. He was carrying a broom and he was about to sweep up the food when he saw the two mice.

He shouted out: "Rover! There are some mice in this pantry! Come on, boy! Catch them!"

The town mouse and the country mouse ran off to hide in a hole. What a huge man! What a nasty lot of noise! The town mouse and the country mouse kept as quiet as mice in their hole. It was dark and cramped but at least it was safe.

When the house was silent again, they came out to eat their dinner. Luckily it was still there. The town mouse took some nuts and  dates, and the country mouse helped himself to cheese and apple.

Then they saw a dog. Its big wet nose came sniffing round the door. It was Rover! He had come to catch them! The town mouse and the country mouse were frightened and lost their appetites at once. So they ran off to hide again.

Poor country mouse! Every time he started
eating, someone came along to frighten him
away. He could not eat
his dinner and he did
not like the town.

The town mouse and the country mouse
waited until the house was quiet again, and then
crept out of the hole.

"My good friend," said the country mouse,
"so much happens in this town. You have lots
of food but you can never eat it in peace! There
are men and dogs coming and going all the
time. This town is too exciting for me! I shall
be on my way."

The country mouse ran all the way back home.
There was his comfortable ditch, and there
was the peaceful countryside all around him. He
had a meal of barleycorn and roots, and then lay
down to rest.

"I may be poor and dull, but at least I can live
here in peace," he said happily.

The End